Meet the Frankencrayon Picture Book Cast and Crew

THE HORRIBLE MONSTER

GREEN
(as the
monster's top)

ORANGE
(as the
monster's middle)

PURPLE
(as the
monster's bottom)

THE FRIGHTENED TOWNSPEOPLE

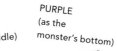

YELLOW

BLACK

TEAL

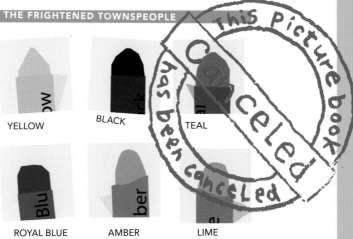

ROYAL BLUE

AMBER

LIME

THE NARRATOR

THE CREW

PENCIL

AZURE

ORCHID

This Picture book has been canceled — CANCELED

Official Notice

This picture book has been canceled. Please close the book and find something else to read.

For Hugh, begrudgingly

Frankencrayon

Copyright © 2016 by Michael Hall • All rights reserved. • Manufactured in China.
For information address HarperCollins Children's Books, a division of HarperCollins
Publishers, 195 Broadway, New York, NY 10007. • www.harpercollinschildrens.com •
The art consists of digitally combined and colored crayon drawings and cut paper.
The text type is 16-point Avenir 55 Roman.

Library of Congress Cataloging-in-Publication Data. Hall, Michael, (date)—author,
illustrator. Frankencrayon / Michael Hall. pages cm "Greenwillow Books."

Summary: "This picture book has been canceled! The crayons are all set to put on
their production of Frankencrayon. All the roles are filled, the costumes are made, and
the curtain is about to go up, when disaster strikes and a scribble is found on the set.
The crayons try their best to erase the scribble, but it just keeps getting bigger and
bigger until it becomes a scribble monster!"—Provided by publisher.

ISBN 978-0-06-225211-1 (hardback)—ISBN 978-0-06-225212-8 (lib. bdg.)
[1. Crayons—Fiction. 2. Monsters—Fiction. 3. Books and reading—Fiction.
4. Humorous stories.] I. Title. PZ7.H1472Fr 2016 [E]—dc23 2015012164

16 17 18 19 SCP 10 9 8 7 6 5 4 3 2 1

First Edition

Greenwillow Books

Michael Hall

Frankencrayon

Canceled

This picture book has been canceled

I can't
believe
it's been
canceled.

It was
my first
starring
role.

It was
my first
supporting
role.

GREENWILLOW BOOKS

An Imprint of HarperCollinsPublishers

Help!
Someone
just
turned
the page.

Take my
hand.

Hey,
someone
must be
reading
this book!

You're
right.
I'll talk
to them.

Ahem...
Hello out there...
I'm sorry to disappoint you,
but this picture book has
been canceled.

Tell
them
what
happened.

Tell
them
about the
scribble.

And don't
leave
anything
out!

Well, let's see... in the beginning, everything went according to plan. The crayons were in their costumes, and I was getting them into position.

Frankencrayon,
go to
page 22.
That's
where
you'll make
your
dramatic
entrance,
just like we
practiced.

I hope
I don't
forget
my lines!

Right.

Got it.

Page 22.

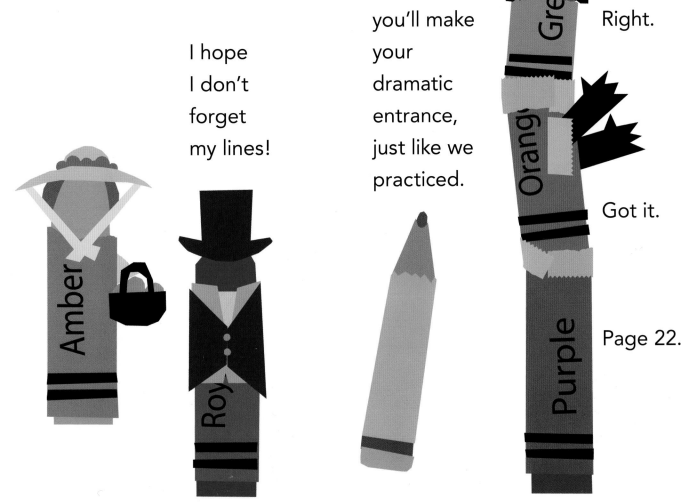

Amber

Roy

Green

Orange

Purple

The story began with
the frightened townspeople
talking about a horrible monster
lurking in their town.

There
is a
horrible
monster
lurking
in our
town!

Oh no!

I'm so
scared!

Suddenly, without warning,
the lights went out.

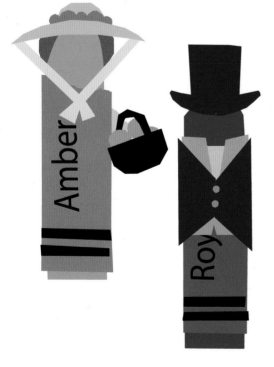

Screeeeeeeeee

eeeeeeeeeetch!

Aaaaa

Amber

aaiiiiieeee!

What is it,
Amber?
What is it?

Someone
turn on
the lights,
please!

It was a scribble.

It went all the way across two pages.

It's horrifying!

Hideous!

Horrendous!

A scribble can ruin a picture book!

Don't worry. We'll take a short break while the crew cleans the page.

But the scribble got bigger.

It's
absolutely
awful!

I think
we made
it worse.

Appalling!

Atrocious!

It's making a mess of our story.

Cast members, we need more help!

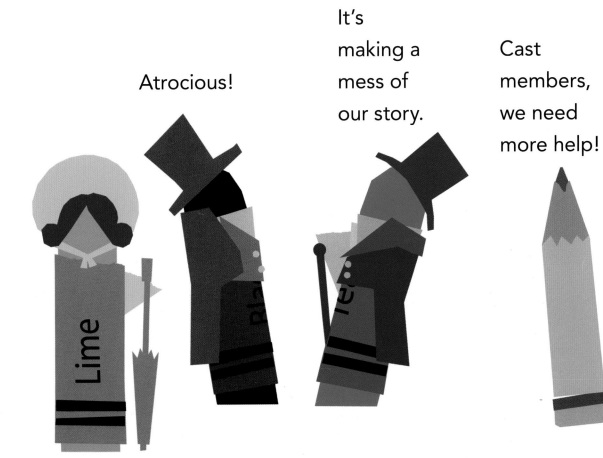

Even four crayons, scrubbing hard, couldn't stop the scribble.

That didn't go well, either.

It's distressing!

Disturbing!

Dreadful!

We need
more help.
Hurry,
please!

But the scribble was out of control.

It's alive!

The story was falling apart.
And that's when the really
terrible news arrived.

Official Notice

We regret to tell you that we've decided to cancel this picture book,

How come? We're almost halfway done.

Official Notice

Because...
1. No one likes the scribble thing.
2. The characters are gone.
3. Isn't there supposed to be a mad scientist in this story?

Yes, but I dropped the mad scientist because he was difficult.

Official Notice

We know you're disappointed, but we ask that you leave this book right away.

What could I do?
I turned out the lights and left.

And that's what happened.

Whoa!
Hang on.
That's not
the whole
story!

You know
what we're
talking
about.

How you
forgot
to tell
us . . .

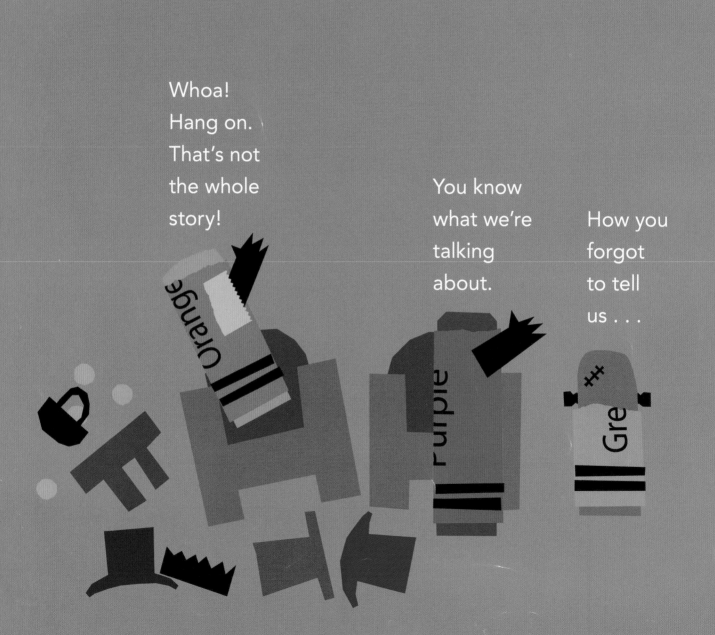

Okay, okay.
Let's see.
Well, I was pretty upset at the time.
And, in my sadness, I forgot to tell
Frankencrayon. So, on page 22...

Rroo

Wait . . .
Where are the
frightened
townspeople?
Isn't this
page 22?

I'll turn on
the lights.

ooaaaarrr . . .

Hello.
Who
are you?

I don't
think it
can talk.

Let's give
it a mouth.
Hop off.

Hello!
I need
to get
moving.
I'm late
for an
important
event.
Can you
help me?

Of course
we can.

It's what
crayons do.

I'll fix you up
in a flash.

Thank you!

What a
beautiful
scribble.

I wish
it didn't
have to
go.

Come on,
let's find the
frightened
townspeople.

Eventually, I came back
to look for the costumes
and found Frankencrayon
eating oranges
in the greenroom.

Where is
everybody?

I have
terrible
news.

We have a
few things to
tell you, too.

I guess that's about it.
We'll probably never know
who scribbled on the page
to begin with. But at least
this has been a learning
experience for all of us

Right.
Lesson
number 1:
Don't
forget
to tell
everyone
when
a story
has been
canceled!

Lesson
number 2:
Don't try to
unscribble
a scribble by
scribbling
on it.

Lesson
number 3:
Even a
messy
scribble
can be a
lovely thing.

Good-bye.

Screeeeeetch!

Wait!
Don't forget
lesson
number 4:
Never drop
the mad scientist
from the
Frankenstein
story!

Official Notice

Mwah ha ha ha!